Jingle Bells

'*T*is Christmas Eve!
Dear Santa Claus will bring
his gifts tonight.
We'll hang our stockings by the bed,
And wait until it's light.
I wonder what he'll bring for you,
And what he'll bring for me.
Ah! There! It's no use wondering,
You'll have to wait and see!

Anon

Jingle Bells

Nick Butterworth

Collins

An Imprint of HarperCollins*Publishers*

CHRISTMAS TIME.
A happy time, or so it should be. Why then, on this Christmas Eve, did two small mice look so unhappy?

"It's That Cat," grumbled Lottie to her brother Jack. "He always spoils things."

Ah, yes. That Cat.

It should have been wonderful for the mice, living in a cart shed on a farm. There were games to play, places to explore and, usually, plenty to eat.

There was only one problem. . . That Cat.

The mice had been hiding food for their Christmas dinner, but the cat had discovered their hiding place.

He didn't particularly like grapes or cheese or cake. But still, he had eaten every bit and left the mice with nothing. That Cat.

"Cheer up," said Jack. "Look what I've found." It was an old glove. Jack began to chew at it.

"We can't eat that," said Lottie.

Jack went on chewing. Soon he had gnawed off two of the glove's fingers.

"There!" he said. "Christmas stockings! One each. We can hang them up for Father Christmas."

"Brilliant!" said Lottie. "I've never had a Christmas stocking."

That night, as the mice snuggled down to sleep, they wondered what Father Christmas would bring them.

Lottie had written their names on a note which she put next to their Christmas stockings, so that Father Christmas would know who they were for.

S oon, Lottie began to snore, Jack began to dream and the air was filled with the sound of sleighbells.

CHRISTMAS MORNING.
The day was fresh and bright as Lottie and Jack hurried excitedly to look at their Christmas stockings.

They were empty.

"Nothing," said Jack sadly. "Not even a nut."

Lottie picked up the note which she had written the night before.

"Look at this!" she said. Underneath their names, someone had written:

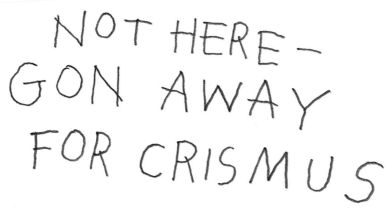

NOT HERE - GON AWAY FOR CRISMUS

"I know who wrote that," said Jack. They both knew.

"It's time we taught That Cat a lesson," said Lottie.

"But what can we do?" said Jack. "He's so big and strong."

"Well," said Lottie, "I think we should go and talk to Ton-Chee."

T on-Chee was a rat. Actually, his real
name was Gavin, but he liked to be
called Ton-Chee.

He wore glasses which had no glass in
them. And he wore clothes which he had
'borrowed' from dolls in the farmhouse
attic.

He also 'borrowed' furniture from
a dolls' house in the attic, which
he said made his own place more homely.

Lottie and Jack made their way through the snow towards the barn where Ton-Chee lived. Suddenly, Jack spotted something. It was shiny and golden.

"It's a bell!" said Jack.

"It's a sleighbell," said Lottie. "It must have fallen off Father Christmas's sleigh. It's lovely. Let's take it with us. We'll show it to Ton-Chee."

When the mice reached the barn they were quite out of breath, but there was still a difficult climb to make.

At last, puffing and panting, they came to a little door at the top of the barn.

Befter Jack could knock, the door
opened.

"Good morning! And a very merry
Christmas to you," said the rat. The mice
smiled and replied nervously. Then they
stepped inside. Ton-Chee shut the door.

It is hard to say exactly what the mice and the rat said to each other. But whatever it was, when the door opened again, all three were smiling.

"Thank you very much," said Lottie and Jack together. Ton-Chee smiled.

"The pleasure is all mine," he said. "Cats can be such a terrible nuisance."

Later, after a Christmas dinner of some 'borrowed' fruitcake which Ton-Chee had given to them, the mice could be seen wrapping up a parcel.

Later still, they tried not to be seen as they cautiously carried their parcel towards the farmhouse.

BOXING DAY.
Mrs Mackie, the farmer's wife swung
her feet out of bed and into her slippers.
At the foot of the stairs, the cat brushed
past her legs.

"Hello, Angus," she said. "What's this?" She picked up a small parcel that lay on the mat and read the label.

"It's an extra present for you Angus!" she said to the cat.

Angus watched as Mrs Mackie opened the parcel. What could it be?

"It's a little bell!" said Mrs Mackie,
"on a pretty red ribbon!"

To Angus
with love
x x x

Before he could escape, Mrs Mackie
took a firm hold of Angus and tied the
ribbon around his neck. The little bell
jingled under his chin.

"There!" she said. "You look lovely!"
Angus twisted his neck uncomfortably
and the bell jingled again.

He pulled a face and pawed at the bell.
"Don't you dare," said Mrs Mackie.
"You keep it on."

It was about tea time in the afternoon. Lottie and Jack were having great fun in the snow. Suddenly they stopped and listened. They could hear the jingling of a little bell.

"Quick! Someone's coming," whispered Lottie.

The mice ran to hide in the cart shed.

As they peered out, they saw a very cross-looking Angus go stalking past. He looked from side to side and shook his head. The little bell jingled merrily.

"Hmmph!" grunted Angus and he stumped off, jingling as he went.

The mice burst into a fit of the giggles and Lottie began to sing.

"Jingle bells, jingle bells, jingle all the way. . .Now Angus can't sneak up on us, when we go out to play!"

They laughed and laughed.

"It may not have been a very merry Christmas," said Jack, "but it does look like being a happy new year!"

First published in Great Britain by HarperCollins Publishers Ltd in 1998

ISBN: 0 00 198315-6

3 5 7 9 10 8 6 4 2

Text and illustrations copyright © Nick Butterworth 1998

The author/illustrator asserts the moral right to be identified
as the author/illustrator of the work.

Manufactured in China by Imago

Nick Butterworth is a designer, artist and author with more than sixty books to his credit. He lives in Suffolk with his wife Annette and their two children, Ben and Amanda.

Nick Butterworth's Percy the Park Keeper stories are available in hardback, paperback and audio cassette:

One Snowy Night • After the Storm
The Rescue Party • The Secret Path • The Treasure Hunt

The Fox's Hiccups • The Cross Rabbit • The Badger's Bath
The Hedgehog's Balloon • One Warm Fox • The Owl's Lesson

A Year in Percy's Park • Tales From Percy's Park

Four Feathers in Percy's Park

Also published by Collins Children's Books

All Together Now!
When We Play Together • When It's Time For Bed
When There's Work To Do • When We Go Shopping
Amanda's Butterfly
THUD!